CAPTAIN UNDERPANTS
AND THE SENSATIONAL SAGA OF
SIR STINKS-A-LOT

The Twelfth Epic Novel by

DAV PILKEY

SCHOLASTIC

A very special thanks to the following people,
who inspired characters in this book: Billy DiMichele,
Meena and Nikhil Willette and the Bhatnagar/Willette family,
Owen and Kei Bernstein and the Geist family

Scholastic Children's Books
An imprint of Scholastic Ltd
Euston House, 24 Eversholt Street
London, NW1 1DB, UK
Registered office: Westfield Road, Southam, Warwickshire, CV47 0RA
SCHOLASTIC and associated logos are trademarks and/or registered
trademarks of Scholastic Inc.

First published in the US by Scholastic Inc., 2015
First published in the UK by Scholastic Ltd, 2015

Copyright © Dav Pilkey, 2015
The right of Dav Pilkey to be identified as the author and
illustrator of this work has been asserted by him.

ISBN 978 1407 13830 5

A CIP catalogue record for this book is available from the British Library.

Printed by CPI Group (UK) Ltd, Croydon, CR0 4YY
Papers used by Scholastic Children's Books are made from
wood grown in sustainable forests.

1 3 5 7 9 10 8 6 4 2

www.scholastic.co.uk

Be sure to check out Dav Pilkey's Extra-crunchy Website O' Fun at
www.pilkey.com

FOR ELLIE BERGER

CHAPTERS

FOREWORD: Captain Underpants: The 100 Per Cent
    True Truth!!!   7

1. George and George and Harold and Harold   13
2. The GOP Guarantee   14
3. The Species Who Knew Too Much   17
4. Smart Earth   20
5. Leggo My Zygo-Gogozizzle 24   25
6. The Trouble with Zizzles   33
7. A Paradox for a Pair of Docs   36
8. Why Can't We Be Fiends?   41
9. Crimes and Mr Meaner   43
10. Spray Day   47
11. ASLS (Attention Superfluous
    Lethargy Syndrome)   53
12. Men at Work   60
13. The Stinky-Kong 2000   65
14. And Now, a Word from Our Sponsor. . .   68
15. Disguise Falling   73
16. Happy Pranksgiving   81
17. Wakey Wakey, Big Mistakey   85
18. Low-Fat Rider   91
19. Let Us Spray   95

20. Away We Go!   102

21. It's Nice to Meet Me   107

22. The Gang's All Here   111

23. Dog Man: The Random Chapter   116

24. Away We Go (Again)!   130

25. It Was Twenty Years Ago Today. . .   133

26. Stinkalicious   135

27. The Incredibly Graphic Violence Chapter,
Part 1 (in Flip-O-Rama™)   139

28. Don't Go Breaking My Spine   150

29. The Incredibly Graphic Violence Chapter,
Part 2 (in Flip-O-Rama™)   153

30. Piqua Prison Blues   162

31. Ooze on Down the Road   165

32. The Night the Lights Went Out in Piqua   171

33. I'm Sendin' Out Good Vibrations   175

34. Laughter Moon Delight   181

35. To Make a Long Story Short   186

36. Stuck in the Puddle with You   187

37. Back to Normal   192

38. Home Again, Naturally   198

39. Meanwhile, Back in the Present. . .   201

CAPTAIN UNDERPANTS:
The 100% True Truth!!!

Once upon a time there was two cool kids named George and Harold.

They were ~~th~~ smart and handsome and stuff.

"Thank you, yes, we know."

"Me too!"

But they had the meanest principal ever. Name of Mr. Krupp.

"Blah Blah Blah!"

One time, Mr. Krupp was being mean.

"You will be my slaves and stuff!"

So they hypnotized him.

"Not today, bub!!!"

Now, whenever Mr. Krupp Hears somebody snap their fingers......

SNAP

...he turns into captain Underpants.

Tra-La Laaaaa!

and whenever Captain Underpants gets water on his head....

...he Turns bAck into Mr. Krupp.

Blah Blah Blah!

So we got **THAT** to deal with.

But it gets **worse!!!**

So they all had to go to the ~~mental~~ mental hospital.

The only **GOOD** thing that happened is that we got three new pets...

They are ½ Bionic hamsters and ½ Pterodactyls.

Orlando

Tony

Dawn

CHAPTER 1

GEORGE AND GEORGE AND HAROLD AND HAROLD

This is George Beard and George Beard and Harold Hutchins and Harold Hutchins. George and George are the kids on the left with the ties and the flat-tops. Harold and Harold are the ones on the right with the T-shirts and the bad haircuts. Remember that now.

CHAPTER 2
THE GOP GUARANTEE*

If you read our last adventure, you're
probably well aware of how George and
Harold accidentally created duplicate versions
of themselves. You know all the whys, the
whens and the wherefores, so you're all
caught up and ready to go. Congratulations!
Good for you. Reading is power, ain't it?

If you *didn't* read our last adventure,
you're probably scratching your head and
saying to yourself, "Hey, myself, what the
heck is going on here?"

*Some restrictions may apply. Void where prohibited.

Before we get into all of that, I should point out that it's impolite to use the word *heck*. These books have been criticized for their inappropriate language, and we're going to put a stop to that sort of thing once and for all. From now on**, you won't be reading any more words like *heck*, or *tinkle*, or *fart*, or *pee-pee*. No, sir! Those words are highly offensive to grouchy old people who have way too much time on their hands.

**Except on pages 44 and 48.

In the interest of pleasing all the grouchy old people (GOP) out there, I have also included topics especially for them. So this adventure will contain references to health care, gardening, Toby Carvery restaurants, hard candies, the Daily Mail and gentle-yet-effective laxatives.

So sit back (on your haemorrhoid pillows), turn up some music (Vera Lynn), and grab a snack (black jelly beans that are all stuck together). It's time to enjoy the all-new, squeaky-clean, fully appropriate and NON-offensive adventures of Captain Underpants!

CHAPTER 3

THE SPECIES WHO KNEW TOO MUCH

We all know that it's good to be smart. It's even better to be *very* smart. But being TOO smart is just asking for trouble. Take human beings for example: We were smart enough to invent gardening and health care, we developed Toby Carvery restaurants and the Daily Mail, and we've managed to take hard candies and gentle-yet-effective laxatives to exciting new horizons. But somewhere along the way, we got TOO smart for our own good. We started inventing dumb things like car alarms, leaf blowers and spray-on hair.

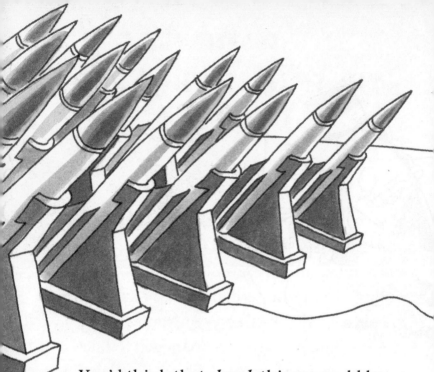

You'd think that *dumb* things would have been good enough for us, but no. Our big, ridiculous brains just weren't satisfied. We had to take things one step further. So we began creating incredibly *dangerous* things like atomic bombs and nuclear warheads, and we built enough of them to wipe out everybody on the planet. Then, like the smarty-pantses we are, we handed the launch codes over to politicians.

Only human beings are smart enough to be that dumb!

It turns out that brains are a lot like beans. They're both good, but you really don't want to overdo it with either one. You see, too much of a good thing usually ends up being a *VERY BAD* thing. One way or another, you're probably going to end up with a big, stinky mess.

The story you are about to read is the unfortunate tale of how the smartest brain on the planet created the biggest, stinkiest mess the world has ever seen. But before I can tell you that story, I have to tell you *this* story. . .

19

CHAPTER 4

SMART EARTH

As any scientist will tell you, we exist in an ever-expanding multiverse with an infinite number of stars and planets.

One of those planets, which orbits around the centre star in Orion's Belt, is called Smart Earth. Smart Earth is almost identical to *our* Earth, except that everybody who lives on Smart Earth is a genius.

The reason everybody on Smart Earth is so smart is that the entire planet is made of an element called Zygo-Gogozizzle 24. Zygo-Gogozizzle 24 is a slightly radioactive substance that can bind with organic matter, morph into complex organisms, and be mixed with mayonnaise and dill-pickle relish to create both a tasty salad dressing and a clean-burning fuel source with enough power to light up an entire city. One of the remarkable side effects of being in close proximity to Zygo-Gogozizzle 24 is that it makes people much, *much* smarter than they normally would be.

Even though Smart Earth is inhabited by geniuses, it still has a lot of similarities to *our* Earth. They've got McDonald's (though it's called "Smart McDonald's"), they have smartphones (which are called "smart smartphones"), and they've got the Huffington Post (which is called "the Huffington Post").

One day, a smart scientist at Smart Harvard University decided to do an experiment.

It was the smartest, most intelligent experiment that anyone on Smart Earth had ever conducted. It was so incredibly smart, in fact, that it ended up being totally dumb.

That afternoon in her laboratory, Smart Earth's smartest scientist mixed Smart Diet Coke with Smart Pop Rocks. Then she added a third ingredient to this highly volatile concoction: Smart Mentos.

This is what happened:

CHAPTER 5

LEGGO MY ZYGO-GOGOZIZZLE 24

The explosion that followed sent chunks of Zygo-Gogozizzle 24 whizzing off in different directions throughout the galaxy and beyond.

One piece of Zygo-Gogozizzle 24 landed in a pond on the nearby planet Badpun, causing all of the pond water to turn into smart pond water.

PLiP

Soon the fish in the pond became *so* intelligent, they started swimming in schools.

Another piece of Zygo-Gogozizzle 24 ended up landing in a grape vineyard on planet Pinot. The Zygo-Gogozizzle 24 was quickly absorbed into the soil and was subsequently soaked up into the grapes.

These grapes, which had until recently been harvested almost to extinction, suddenly became self-aware and super intelligent. They banded together in bunches and rose up to defeat their oppressors.

The battle lasted one whole night, but sadly, it ended the next morning when the sun came up. The rebellion shrivelled when the poor grapes ran out of juice. Apparently, there's a raisin for everything.

Perhaps the most devastating result of the destruction of Smart Earth, however, occurred when a tiny piece of Zygo-Gogozizzle 24 entered our *own* planet's atmosphere. It soared down through the sky at a terrific speed, zooming closer and closer to the small midwestern town of Piqua, Ohio.

Finally, the tiny chunk of Zygo-Gogozizzle 24 crashed through the roof of the Piqua Valley Home for the Reality-Challenged. It landed in the group-therapy ward, where all of the teachers from the nearby elementary school had recently been transferred.

"What's that?" cried Mr Krupp.

"Looks like a meteorite," said Ms Ribble.

"Don't touch it," warned the doctor. "It might be *the Blob*!"

The doctor's warning was heeded by everyone except for the gym teacher, Mr Meaner. Gym teachers, as I'm sure you are all aware, are a lot like toddlers. You really have to keep an eye on them, because they're always picking things up off the floor and putting them in their mouths.

Unfortunately, that's exactly what happened on that fateful day at the Piqua Valley Home for the Reality-Challenged.

"Mmmmmm," said Mr Meaner, as he happily chewed up the Zygo-Gogozizzle 24 and swallowed hard. "Tastes like chicken!"

CHAPTER 6
THE TROUBLE WITH ZIZZLES

Suddenly, the tiny chunk of Zygo-Gogozizzle 24 began to bind with Mr Meaner's stomach lining. It started taking over his cells at an alarming rate, spreading throughout his squishy innards and overriding his normal bodily functions. Soon, the Zygo-Gogozizzle 24 reached Mr Meaner's mind, where it supercharged all of his brain cells and began the complicated process of making him smart.

"Are you all right, Mr Meaner?" asked the psychologist. "You look a little strange."

"I'm much more than *all right*," replied Mr Meaner. "I'm exceptionally impeccable!"

Mr Meaner's fellow teachers looked worried. They had never heard him use anything larger than a three-syllable word before. Usually, Mr Meaner just pointed at things and grunted.

"Er, I think you'd better sit down," said the psychologist.

"Nonsense, my good man," said Mr Meaner, as his mind's neurons and glial cells began restructuring themselves, forming new connections and making his brain smarter and smarter each second. "I've wasted far too much time in this insipid infirmary already."

"Now, wait just a minute," said the psychologist. "You can't leave here. You're a patient."

"On the contrary," said Mr Meaner, who now spoke in a standard British accent. "I shall walk right out that door expeditiously, and neither you nor anyone else is going to stop me."

"HELP! EMERGENCY!" shouted the psychologist. "We've got a runner!"

Another doctor rushed in to help. Together, the two doctors blocked the exit and refused to budge.

"You're not going anywhere, bub!" said the psychologist.

Mr Meaner smirked as he looked at the two doctors with pity. This was going to be *too easy*.

CHAPTER 7

A PARADOX FOR A PAIR OF DOCS

Mr Meaner approached the two doctors.

"I have some advice for both of you," said Mr Meaner.

"Well, too bad," said the psychologist. "Because we're not going to follow *any* of your advice!"

"Is that so?" asked Mr Meaner. "Then I advise you to *NOT* follow my advice!"

The two doctors were confused.

"W-Well, we're *not* going to follow that advice," said the psychologist.

"But if we *don't* follow his advice to *not* follow his advice," said the other doctor, "then aren't we *following* his advice?"

"Wait a minute," said the psychologist. "What if we follow his advice to *NOT* follow his advice? Are we still following his advice?"

The two doctors became so entangled in their deep, paradoxical conversation that they didn't even notice Mr Meaner walking out the exit door.

"Hey, now's our chance to escape, too," said Ms Ribble. The other teachers followed her out the door, right past the increasingly confused and frustrated doctors.

All of the teachers and staff of Jerome Horwitz Elementary School were now free. They followed Mr Meaner up to the hilltop and watched him in awe as he looked out over the horizon.

Most people in Mr Meaner's position would use their newfound genius brains to end world hunger and bring peace to humanity. But these were the last things on Mr Meaner's magnificent mind.

Mr Meaner was still a gym teacher at heart, you see. And as everyone knows, most gym teachers are inherently evil.

CHAPTER 8

WHY CAN'T WE BE FIENDS?

"It occurs to me," said Mr Meaner, "that our recent problems have all been caused by wilful and disobedient children."

"I heard that!" said Mr Krupp.

"SILENCE, YOU FOOL!" Mr Meaner shouted. "If we are to rectify this aberration, we must proceed with prudence and acumen!"

"I'm not sure what those words mean," said Miss Anthrope, "but I agree one hundred and thirty-nine per cent!"

"Me, too," said the other teachers simultaneously.

"Then you must follow my every command," said Mr Meaner. "You must all return to your jobs and go about your business as usual. Nothing is to look suspicious."

"B-But we want to be evil, too," Mr Rected whined.

"Patience, my dear minions," said Mr Meaner with a hideous sneer. "There will be plenty of time for that in the days to come!"

CHAPTER 9
CRIMES AND MR MEANER

A few days later, school was back in session.
The teachers taught, the students studied . . .

. . . and George and Harold went back to their mischief.

After school, George and Harold climbed up into their tree house to do their homework. The "yesterday" versions of themselves were busy playing video games and reading comics.

"How was school today?" asked Yesterday George.

"Meh," said George.

"Didja learn anything new?" asked Yesterday Harold.

"Eh," said Harold, shrugging.

By all appearances, things had finally returned to normal.

But at night, Mr Meaner tinkered away at a makeshift laboratory inside an old, abandoned factory near Franz Pond. He was developing a powerful mind-control potion that would turn even the most unruly child into a brainlessly obedient conformist.

Using a base mixture of sodium thiopental, Mr Meaner added liberal doses of butyric acid, tryptophan and Clamato juice. Then he filtered the solution through an old, dirty pile of stinky gym socks. The concoction smelled terrible, but its sinister effect would be even worse!

"My formula is now ready for human trials," said Mr Meaner. "And I know exactly *which two humans* I'm going to try it out on!"

CHAPTER 10
SPRAY DAY

The next day, Mr Meaner showed up at school looking a little different than usual. He still wore the same smelly sweatshirt and sweatpants he'd had on all week – nothing new there – but somehow, something about him had changed.

It was Yesterday George and Yesterday Harold's turn to go to school and do homework that day, so the boys dutifully went to their classes and did everything they were supposed to do . . .

JOIN US FOR WEDNESDAY'S "MATH CHAT"

. . . and a few things they were *not* supposed to do.

Everything seemed normal until after gym class. Mr Meaner excused the rest of the kids, but not Yesterday George and Yesterday Harold.

"Boys," said Mr Meaner, "I'd like to see you in my office, pronto!"

"Why?" asked Yesterday George. "We didn't do anything–*probably*."

Mr Meaner pointed to his office door. "IN–MY–OFFICE–NOW!" he shouted.

49

Yesterday George and
Yesterday Harold slinked into Mr Meaner's
filthy office. They'd been in there before, and
they hated the smell of it. It reeked of mould,
rat urine and the putrid sweat of a thousand
tormented souls. But today, for some strange
reason, it smelled even *worse* than usual.

Yesterday George and Yesterday Harold
climbed into two sticky vinyl chairs and held
their breath.

50

"Well, well, well," said Mr Meaner, as he closed the door behind him and approached our heroes. "It looks like we're alone at last."

"What's going on here?" asked Yesterday George suspiciously.

"Yeah," said Yesterday Harold. "We've got to go to our next class."

"Oh, there will be plenty of time for classes and studying and homework," replied Mr Meaner. "But first, I'd like you to help me out with a little experiment!"

Mr Meaner lifted his arms, revealing two metallic spray nozzles under his crusty pits.

"Say hello to my stinky friends!" He laughed as the nozzles spattered out two brown cloudbursts of choking, noxious stank.

CHAPTER 11

ASLS
(ATTENTION SUPERFLUOUS
LETHARGY SYNDROME)

You've probably all heard of ADHD. It's
a condition known as Attention Deficit
Hyperactivity Disorder. George and Harold
had been diagnosed with it when they were
in the second grade.

At the time, George's dad had explained to
the boys that people with ADHD are usually
more creative than ordinary people. This
made George and Harold feel very special,
and they wore their diagnosis like a badge
of honour.

THE
TRUTH
AbouT
ADHD

But today, as they walked down the hallway to their next class, the boys felt much different than normal. It was almost as if their ADHD had been dramatically *reversed* somehow. They felt focused and attentive. They were calm and orderly. They did not feel the uncontrollable urge to daydream or misbehave. Something had changed about them.

"YOU'RE LATE FOR CLASS!" shouted their math teacher, Anita Calculator.

"We are very sorry." said Yesterday Harold robotically.

"Just for that, I'm going to give you *EXTRA* homework!" Miss Calculator snarled.

"Thank you, dear teacher." said Yesterday George in an enthusiastic monotone. "That would be lovely!"

Miss Calculator eyed the two boys suspiciously as they found their way to their desks and sat down quietly. All through class, as she droned on and on, she observed the most peculiar thing she had ever seen. Yesterday George and Yesterday Harold were actually *sitting still and paying attention*. They weren't fidgeting, they weren't giggling and they weren't drawing or talking or making irritating noises with their armpits. They had become *model students*.

"I don't know what you two boys are up to," said Miss Calculator at the end of class, "but I LIKE it!"

"Thank you." said Yesterday George.
"Our greatest desire is to please you."

"That is right." said Yesterday Harold.
"And thank you for all the extra
homework, too. We will do our very
best!"

Even Melvin Sneedly was impressed.
"Those guys are cooler than I thought,"
said Melvin.

All through the day, Yesterday George and Yesterday Harold were making quite an impression on the staff of Jerome Horwitz Elementary School. The teachers couldn't believe it when the two boys walked right past a bulletin board without changing the letters around.

"They could have easily rearranged those letters to read: *Our Cafeteria Makes You Barf*," said Ms Guided. "But they didn't!"

"I don't know what's going on with those two kids," said Miss Labler, "but I LIKE it!"

TRY OUR CAFETERIA'S FUN "MAKE-A-TACO" BAR!

At the end of the school day, Yesterday George and Yesterday Harold went around to each classroom, asking if they could do extra-credit homework that evening. The teachers gladly piled it on.

"I don't know what you did to those two brats today," said Mr Krupp, "but I LIKE it!"

"This is only the beginning," Mr Meaner sneered. "Today I changed George and Harold. Soon, I shall change the world!"

Unlike most megalomaniacs, Mr Meaner had no interest in taking over the planet. He was smarter than that. He knew that the *real* money and power was in pharmaceuticals. Mr Meaner had created a formula that transformed children into highly attentive, obedient slaves. All he needed to do was mass market his creation, and he would become the most powerful entity on Earth.

"Adults will pay through the NOSE for that kind of thing," he said with a laugh, petting Mr Krupp's head affectionately. "But for now, the first taste is free."

CHAPTER 12
MEN AT WORK

That afternoon, Yesterday George and Yesterday Harold climbed up into the tree house with so much homework, they had to make two trips to hoist it all up.

"WHOA!" shouted George. "What happened today?!!?"

"It was a great day." said Yesterday Harold. "The teachers were so kind, they gave us seventeen pounds of homework!"

"SEVENTEEN POUNDS OF HOMEWORK?!!?" shouted Harold. "WE'RE *DOOMED*!"

"No, we are not," said Yesterday George. "We can all work on it together. It will be *fun*!"

George and Harold looked at each other in horror. Never in a million years would they have used the words *homework* and *fun* in the same sentence. Something was wrong. Something was terribly, terribly wrong.

"Are you thinking what I'm thinking?" whispered George.

"Body snatchers," whispered Harold.

"Yep," whispered George.

The four boys sat at their table and began tackling their assignments. Yesterday George and Yesterday Harold ploughed through page after page of worksheets and take-home quizzes at a dizzying rate. George and Harold tried to keep up, but they kept getting distracted.

At supper time, Yesterday George and Yesterday Harold went down to their homes to eat with their families. An hour later, they went back up to the tree house to continue their work.

"We brought some extra food for you." said Yesterday Harold.

"Thanks," said George and Harold.

Everyone worked until it was time for bed.

"We have completed our half to the best of our ability." said Yesterday George.

George and Harold hadn't even made a dent in their half.

"We're gonna be working on this all night!" moaned Harold.

"I have a satisfactory suggestion." said Yesterday George. "You two boys finish your work tonight, and we will go to school again tomorrow."

"Really?" said George. "You'll go to school *TWO DAYS IN A ROW*?!!?"

"Nobody should have to endure *that*," cried Harold.

"We do not mind." said Yesterday George and Yesterday Harold simultaneously. "We LOVE school!"

So while Yesterday George and Yesterday Harold slept in their beds, George and Harold stayed up until 5:00 A.M. answering questions, filling in blanks, and showing their work.

"Man, I'm wiped out!" said George. "If this keeps up, we're going to get sick."

"I'm already getting sick," said Harold, as he blew his nose.

CHAPTER 13

THE STINKY-KONG 2000

The next day, Mr Meaner looked even *more* different than he had the day before. He'd been building a mechanical ape suit in his laboratory, and each new morning it got more and more elaborate. The genius gym teacher started the day by spraying all of the children in his classes with his newest mind-control formula, Rid-O-Kid 2000™.

"Say hello to my stinky friends!" shouted Mr Meaner with each squirt.

In no time at all, the entire student body of Jerome Horwitz Elementary School was transformed. Now *every* kid in school had Attention Superfluous Lethargy Syndrome.

"This is WONDERFUL!" Mr Krupp exclaimed. "There's no more laughing, no more daydreaming and no more running or playing or goofing around. It's like you've crushed their spirits *AND* their imaginations in one fell swoop!"

"I'm really doing the world a great service," Mr Meaner said with a slithery smile. "I'm raising a new generation of totally compliant button-pushers. They'll do what they're told, they won't question authority, and best of all, NO COMPLAINING!"

"Yeah, but isn't Rid-O-Kid 2000™ dangerous?" asked Ms Ribble.

"Not for us," said Mr Meaner. "The spray only affects children. Adults are totally immune, so it's perfectly safe!"

The only downside to Mr Meaner's intra-nasally absorbed spray is that it only lasted for twenty-four hours. To be completely effective, it needed to be resprayed every day.

"That's the beauty of my system," said Mr Meaner. "Once parents see how easy it is to control children, they'll pay ANYTHING for a daily *fix*!"

CHAPTER 14

AND NOW, A WORD FROM OUR SPONSOR...

As the week progressed, George and Harold got more and more swamped with homework. They stayed up later and later each night and got sicker and sicker.

"Let's take a break and watch some TV," said George one morning, as he wiped his nose.

"OK," said Harold, with a sneeze.

George turned on the TV and flipped through the channels. Suddenly, he saw a familiar face.

"HEY!" shouted Harold. "That's Mr Meaner!"

"What's *HE* doing on TV?" cried George. He turned up the volume, and the two boys watched Mr Meaner's commercial in horror.

Are your kids annoying?

Do they fight and whine and complain all the time?

Do they refuse to eat anything but macaroni and cheese?

Are they sucking the LIFE out of you?

Well, RID-O-KID 2000™ is here to help.

Our scientifically proven formula will transform even the most wilful child into an obedient, respectful and hardworking slave – er, I mean, angel.

And RID-O-KID 2000™ has a full day's supply of Vitamin C, so you can feel GOOD about dosing your child with a narcotic that has never been tested for long-term effects.

So turn your brat into a brown-noser . . . with RID-O-KID 2000™.

"I KNEW something was wrong," said Harold, "but it looks even worse than I'd imagined!"

"We'd better go to school and get to the bottom of this!" said George.

"But we're sick," cried Harold. "I can't even breathe through my nose!"

"Me neither," said George. "But a kid's gotta do what a kid's gotta do!"

CHAPTER 15

DISGUISE FALLING

George and Harold rummaged through their houses until they found what they needed. There was no way they were going to show up at school looking like *themselves* again. They'd learned that lesson in our last book. George and Harold needed a disguise, and it needed to be convincing.

When they arrived at school, George
changed into his costume behind the bushes
and climbed on to Harold's shoulders. Then
they headed into the building. Normally,
any stranger entering Jerome Horwitz
Elementary School would need to sign
in at the office and go through a security
screening. But George and Harold noticed
that things at school were a little more
relaxed today.

Their first clue was that there were no adults in the office. At least it looked that way. Upon closer inspection, they discovered that the school secretary, Miss Anthrope, was sound asleep on the floor under her desk. Some third graders were giving her a foot massage, while the sixth-grade AV club was answering the phone and filing papers.

"That's weird," said George.

As George and Harold walked down the hallway, things just got weirder and weirder. First, they noticed a brownish haze in the air.

"I wonder what that brown fog is all about," said George.

"I don't know," said Harold. "I can't smell a thing because of my cold."

"Me neither," said George.

As they roamed from room to room, they noticed that the other teachers were asleep, too, and their students were doing all sorts of odd things for them. Some kids were giving the teachers massages, and others were shaving their teachers' beards, plucking their eyebrows and giving them haircuts.

The mathletes were filling out the
teachers' tax forms, while the shop kids were
washing all the cars in the staff parking lot.

Finally, George and Harold reached the cafeteria, where several teachers were lying on the lunch tables getting Ashiatsu massages and mani-pedis at the same time.

"Boy, things sure have got a lot better around this place since Rid-O-Kid 2000™ came along!" said Ms Zurry.

"I'll say," said Ms Guided. "I was happy enough when my students were finally able to sit still and pay attention all day. But when I found out that they'd follow my every command without question, it changed my life!"

"Mine, too," said Mr Rected. "I just sent my whole class over to my home. They're mowing my lawn, watering my garden and painting my house as we speak!"

The three teachers all had a good laugh and drifted off into a relaxing, dreamy sleep.

"Oh, NO!" cried Harold. "The teachers have turned all the kids into mindless slaves! We'd better get out of here before they turn *us* into slaves, too."

"OK," said George, with a wicked smile.
"But first, let's have a little fun."

CHAPTER 16
HAPPY PRANKSGIVING

"If all the kids in school are blindly following the orders of adults," said George, "then maybe they'll follow OUR orders, too, since we're *dressed* like an adult."

"That makes sense," said Harold. "Let's order everyone to *STOP* following orders!"

"Nah," said George. "We've already used that joke in this book. I've got a better idea!"

So George and Harold went around the school whispering *NEW* orders to all of the students. First, they whispered some new orders to the kids who were giving out free shaves and haircuts.

"Are you sure?" asked the children.

"Of course I'm sure," said George. "I'm an authority figure!"

"Very well, sir." said the children.

Next, they whispered some new orders to the kids who were filling out tax forms.

"Are you sure?" asked the children.

"I'm an adult!" said George. "Don't question me!"

"All right, sir." said the children.

Then they passed out permanent markers to another group of kids, and whispered some new orders to them, too.

"Are you SURE?" asked the children.

"Absolutely!" said George. "I'm a grown-up. I don't make mistakes!"

"As you wish." said the children.

The rest of the afternoon continued in much the same way, with George and Harold dishing out new orders to every kid they came across.

"We'd better get out of here," said Harold. "Those teachers are going to wake up pretty soon, and they're not going to be very happy!"

"OK," said George. "We can do the last one on our way home."

As they headed back to their tree house, George and Harold stopped by Mr Rected's place. His whole garden was filled with children mowing the lawn, watering the flower garden and painting the house. George whispered some new orders to them as well.

"Are you SURE?!!?" asked the children.

"Sure, we're sure," said George. "I mean, 'Sure, *I'M* sure.' Don't use your brains. Just follow orders!"

CHAPTER 17

WAKEY WAKEY, BIG MISTAKEY

George and Harold walked back to their tree house feeling pretty good about themselves. But things were not looking so good for the teachers at school, who were just waking up.

"Hey!" shouted Miss Anthrope. "Somebody drew on my face with permanent markers while I was asleep!"

"Mine, too!" shouted Miss Fitt. "And they spray-painted my *rear end*!"

"Someone gave me a Mohawk!" cried Ms Ribble.

"Somebody shaved off my eyebrows and *Goofy-Glued* them to my chin!" wailed Ms Zurry.

"Somebody filled out my tax forms in *pig Latin* and mailed them to the IRS!" screamed Miss Labler.

Ms Dayken rushed to the mirror. "Thank goodness nobody did anything to me." She laughed. "Hooray!"

"Don't look now," cried Mr Rustworthy, "but a bunch of kids are out in the parking lot filling up our cars with low-fat cottage cheese!"

The teachers all rushed to the windows.

"WHAT IS THE MEANING OF THIS?!!!?" they shouted.

"We are following orders." said one of the children.

"WHO GAVE YOU THOSE ORDERS?" screamed Mr Krupp.

"An authority figure." said another kid. "We *never* question authority figures."

The teachers were outraged. They marched across town to the old, abandoned building that Mr Meaner had converted into a Rid-O-Kid 2000™ spray-can factory.

"LOOK WHAT THOSE KIDS DID TO US!" Mr Krupp shouted at Mr Meaner. "That stupid, stinky spray of yours doesn't work!"

"That's impossible," said Mr Meaner. "I'm going to get to the bottom of this."

90

CHAPTER 18
LOW-FAT RIDER

Mr Meaner ran back to school, climbed into his low-fat-cottage-cheese-filled car, and drove around the city. Even with his massive, intelligent brain, he still couldn't figure out what had gone wrong.

As he drove, he passed by a curious sight.
A group of children were watering someone's
house, mowing their flower garden, and
painting their lawn. Mr Meaner stopped his
car and got out.

"What on *EARTH* are you children doing?" he asked.

"We are following orders." said one of the kids.

"Who *ordered* you to do these things?" asked Mr Meaner.

"A grown-up." said the kid. "Grown-ups do not make mistakes."

Mr Meaner squished back into his car and peeled off.

"No adult would give those kinds of orders," Mr Meaner concluded. "This HAS to be the work of a *CHILD*. And there's only one way to solve *that* problem!"

Mr Meaner zoomed back to his factory and strapped himself into the Stinky-Kong 2000 Mecha-Suit he had been building all week.

"Somewhere in this town there are *children* hiding," Mr Meaner said, "and I'm gonna *GIT* 'em!"

CHAPTER 19
LET US SPRAY

The genius gym teacher stomped out of his factory and headed down the street, spraying everything in sight with his hideous Mecha-Spray Armpits.

"SAY HELLO TO MY STINKY FRIENDS!" he shouted.

The horrible brown clouds rose up over the city, getting bigger and billowier as they spread out across the town. After several hours, George and Harold could see the brown clouds from their tree house window.

"There's that brown fog again," said George. "It won't be long before it reaches *our* neighbourhood!"

"It's a good thing our noses are clogged up," said Harold. "We can't smell it, so we're immune."

"Yeah, but our colds won't last for ever," said George. "I'm already starting to feel better."

"Uh-oh," said Harold. "We need to find an adult we can trust, and FAST!"

George and Harold had no other choice but to ask their parents for help. The two desperate boys sneaked into Harold's house, where both of their families were sitting together, just finishing up dinner.

"Thanks for inviting us over for supper," said George's dad.

"It's always a pleasure," said Harold's mum.

"Please let us clear the table." said Yesterday George.

"What a splendid idea." said Yesterday Harold. "Then we shall wash the dishes and mop the floor! Oh, what fun we shall have!"

George and Harold hid in the hallway, waiting for just the right moment to come in and tell everyone their terrible tale of woe. But before they got a chance, their parents began to talk.

"I don't know what's come over those two boys lately," said George's dad, "but I LIKE it!"

"Me, too," said Harold's mum. "They've really grown up these past few days."

"It's like their whole personalities have changed," said George's mum. "What an *improvement*!"

George and Harold looked at each other with sadness . . .

. . . then walked back to their tree house, broken-hearted.

"Aw, man," said Harold. "Our parents like the *new* versions of us better than they like the *us* versions of us."

"We're going to have to find some adults we can REALLY trust," said George.

"But who?" cried Harold.

"I've got an idea," said George.

George and Harold ran across town
through the choking brown fog until they
reached Melvin Sneedly's house. Luckily,
Melvin's garage door was open. Even
luckilier, Melvin's glow-in-the-dark, time-
travelling Robo-Squid suits were there, too.

George climbed up into one of the cockpits
and fired up the engine. The Robo-Squid
suit lunged forward and grabbed Harold in
its tentacled arm. Then it slithered down the
pavement while George set the controllers.

"You know, we really shouldn't be taking this," said Harold. "It isn't ours."

"Technically, it *IS* ours," said George. "Melvin only had *one* of these things, and WE made the second one. You can't *steal* something you made yourself, can you?"

"That's a good point," said Harold.

George finished setting the controllers and pressed the "Start" button. The Robo-Squid suit shook and sputtered, then disappeared into a ball of blinding light.

CHAPTER 20

AWAY WE GO!

George and Harold were instantly transported twenty years into the future. Quickly, they ran up to an old lady sitting with her twenty-three-year-old son.

"Look, son," said the old lady. "A giant, glow-in-the-dark robotic squid is carrying a little boy in one of its tentacles!"

"*Sure* it is, Mum," said her son. "Listen, you need to take your medication EVERY DAY or it's not going to—"

"Excuse me," said George.

The twenty-three-year-old looked up from his phone and screamed, "AAAAAH! IT'S A GIANT, GLOW-IN-THE-DARK ROBOTIC SQUID CARRYING A LITTLE BOY IN ONE OF ITS TENTACLES!"

"Uh, yeah," said George. "Look, we need to borrow your mobile phone. We're trying to locate George Beard."

"You mean the author?" said the guy.

"D-Did you say *AUTHOR*?!!?" cried George excitedly.

"Yeah," said the guy. "Everybody knows George Beard. He writes those Dog Man graphic novels."

"NO WAY!!!" screamed George. He was so overcome with happiness, he couldn't contain himself. The glow-in-the-dark, time-travelling Robo-Squid suit jumped up and down, spun around and danced a happy jig. "I WRITE GRAPHIC NOVELS IN THE FUTURE!!!" screamed George. "OH YEAH!!! I WRITE GRAPHIC NOVELS IN THE FUTURE!!!"

"Settle down," cried Harold, who was starting to feel ill from all the dancing and jerking around. "You're acting too crazy, man. Show a little self-control, OK?!!?"

"Sorry," said George, setting Harold down.

"Do you know where Mr Beard lives?" George asked the guy.

"Yeah, he lives up there on Echo Hills next to that graphic novel artist," said the guy. "I think his name is . . . um . . . Harold *Hutchings* or something."

"*I'M* HAROLD HUTCHINGS OR
SOMETHING!" screamed Harold, as he
jumped up and down, flipped somersaults
and ran around in circles like a crazy person.
"I ILLUSTRATE GRAPHIC NOVELS IN
THE FUTURE! OH BABY!!! I ILLUSTRATE
GRAPHIC NOVELS IN THE FUTURE!"

"C'mon, *Mr Self-Control*," said George.
"Let's go meet our future selves!"

CHAPTER 21
IT'S NICE TO MEET ME

George and Harold could hardly contain themselves as they rang the doorbell of George's future self. They were so excited, they'd almost forgotten why they had come to the future in the first place.

Soon, George's future self came to the door. He looked a lot like George, only he was really, really old. He was almost *THIRTY*!

Old George recognized George and Harold immediately.

"HOLY *TOLEDO*!" cried Old George. "Wh-What are *you guys* doing here?"

Old George's wife came to the door, too. "Don't be rude to your fans, honey," she said. "Invite them in! Make yourselves at home, boys."

"These aren't my fans, dear," said Old George. "They're US!"

"US *who*?" asked Mrs Beard.

"It's Harold and me from when we were kids," said Old George.

George and Harold accepted Mrs Beard's invitation and made themselves right at home. They gleefully tore through the house, checking out all of Old George's stuff.

"Your future house is *AWESOME*!" said Harold.

"Thanks," said George. "I must admit, I have pretty good taste!"

"WOW!" cried Harold. "You've even got your own PINBALL MACHINE!!!"

"COOL!" exclaimed George. "I've always wanted one!"

"Can I play it?" asked Harold.

"I guess so," said George. "After all, it's *mine*."

"Look, Harold," cried George. "There's even a tree house in my back garden!"

"Er, that's not for *us*," said Old George. "That's for our kids."

"Our *KIDS*?!!?" asked George.

"I guess it's time you boys met the whole family," said Mrs Beard. "I'll go round up the children, honey, while you call Harold and Billy."

CHAPTER 22

THE GANG'S ALL HERE

Soon, everyone had gathered together in Old George's studio. Old George, his wife and their kids, Meena and Nik, sat on the sofa, while Old Harold, his husband and their twins, Owen and Kei, plopped down in the giant beanbag chair.

"Kids," said Mrs Beard, "I'd like you to meet your fathers."

"What's up?" said George.

"We're your dads when they were kids," said Harold.

"Wow, Dad," said Meena. "You used to be cute!"

"Whaddaya mean, *used to be*?!!?" said Old George.

"We're here because we need to borrow your dads," said Harold. "They're the only adults we can trust!"

"Yeah," said George. "It's a real emergency!"

"Wait a minute," said Old Harold. "I don't remember doing any of this when we were kids, do you, George?"

"No," said Old George. "If *this* happened in our past, how come *we* have no memory of it?"

"I don't know," said Harold.

"Probably bad writing," said George.

"Well, if we're going to help you, we'd better get going," said Old George. "Let's boogie!"

"But wait," said Harold. "We need to finish our pinball game."

"Yeah," said George. "And we haven't even read your graphic novels yet."

"I thought this was an *emergency*," said Old Harold.

"How about just ONE chapter?" Harold begged. *"Pleeeeeease?"*

"Well, all right," said Old Harold.

George and Harold grabbed a graphic
novel from the bookshelf, flipped it open, and
started reading from a random chapter.

CHAPTER 23
DOG MAN: THE RANDOM CHAPTER

NO, DOG MAN NO! BAD DOG MAN!

HOW COULD YOU BETRAY US LIKE THIS, DOG MAN?

OOG MAN S THE ONE VHO IS DEAD. . .

ZNNNNP!

MY VENUS-FLYTRAP MONKEYS HAVE SURELY FINISHED HIM OFF BY NOW!

CHONG

AND NOW, DEAR COPPERS, IT IS *YOUR* TURN TO DIE!

HEY, YOU BROKE MY SWORD!

YOU OWE ME SIXTEEN BUCKS!

D'YA GIVE UP, OR D'YA WANT SOME MORE?

MY MASK!

HEY! YOU'RE NOT MECHA-PETEY!

NO! THIS WHOLE TIME IT'S BEEN ME: PORKBELLY! THE WORLD'S MOST SINISTER PSYCHOKINETIC ANGELFISH!

PORKBELLY?!!? I THOUGHT HE WAS DEAD!

THAT'S WHAT I *WANTED* YOU TO THINK!

TO BE CONTINUED. . .

CHAPTER 24
AWAY WE GO (AGAIN)!

"Well?" said Old George. "What did you think? Did you like it?"

"I guess so," said Harold.

"Yeah," said George. "It was pretty good— for old people."

"PRETTY GOOD?!!?" cried Old Harold.

"OLD PEOPLE?!!?" cried Old George.

"All right, let's boogie!" said George, as he went to the front garden and powered up the Robo-Squid suit. Quickly, he reached out three mechanical arms and picked up Harold, Old Harold and Old George.

Suddenly, everything began to shake and sputter as a massive ball of electric light enveloped them all.

"Are you guys ready to go?" asked Harold.

"PRETTY GOOD?!!?" whined Old Harold.

"OLD PEOPLE?!!?" whined Old George.

As our heroes began to disappear into the shifting paradigms of time, they waved goodbye to their frightened families.

"Don't worry, kids," shouted George. "We'll all be back by chapter 38!"

CHAPTER 25

IT WAS TWENTY YEARS AGO TODAY...

Everything stopped suddenly, and George, Harold and their future selves looked down from the vacant hilltop. They were back in the present, and the entire city below them was surrounded by a gigantic, stinky brown cloud.

Quickly, they made their way through the dark clouds to their tree house.

"WOW!" cried Old George. "I haven't been up here in years."

"Look," cried Old Harold. "It's Tony, Orlando and Dawn. I remember them!"

"Yeah, whatever happened to them?" said Old George. "It was like they just *disappeared* one day!"

"I don't know what you're talking about," said Harold. "They've always been here, ever since they hatched."

"Listen, boys," said Old George. "You need to stay up here. We'll take care of Mr Meaner and his stinky gas."

"Yeah," said Old Harold. "It's up to the *adults* to save the world this time!"

CHAPTER 26
STINKALICIOUS

The first thing that Old George and Old Harold did was run to Mr Krupp's house.

Unfortunately, Mr Meaner was walking down Mr Krupp's street at that very moment in his Stinky-Kong 2000 Mecha-Suit, blowing brown, putrid fog throughout the neighbourhood. Old George rang Mr Krupp's doorbell, panicking. Suddenly, Mr Krupp swung the front door open. He'd been at his kitchen sink all evening, scrubbing the permanent marker off of his face.

"What do *YOU* people want?!!?" shouted Mr Krupp.

"We need the help of an old friend," said Old Harold, snapping his fingers.

"WELL?!!?" Mr Krupp screamed. *"ANSWER ME!!!"*

Old George and Old Harold looked at each other in shock.

"It didn't work!" cried Old Harold. They both snapped their fingers this time.

SNAP! SNAP! SNAP! SNAP! SNAP! SNAP!

"HEY!" Mr Krupp screamed. "Quit snapping your fingers in my face, you weirdos!"

Mr Meaner and his Stinky-Kong 2000 Mecha-Suit were getting closer.

The whole street shook with every forceful stomp of his metallic monkey feet. Old George and Old Harold continued snapping their fingers feverishly.

"Why isn't it working?" cried Old Harold as he snapped.

"It must be all that water that's on his face!" cried Old George. "That's gotta be what's keeping him from transforming!"

"LISTEN UP, YOU TWO *PSYCHOS*!" Mr Krupp screamed. "You better get outta my garden before I call the COPS! You're supposed to be ADULTS, but you're acting like a couple of KIDS!"

Suddenly, Mr Meaner stopped. *"Adults acting like kids?"* he said, turning his head slyly. He looked at Old George and Old Harold. His genius brain began to calculate rapidly as he eyed them up and down. Then his face widened with a sinister, foul-smelling smile.

"Adults who act like children would be immune to my Rid-O-Kid 2000™ spray," Mr Meaner said. "So *THEY* must be the pranksters I've been looking for!"

Mr Meaner stomped up to Old George and Old Harold, and grabbed the two friends in the clenching claws of the Stinky-Kong 2000.

CHAPTER 27

THE INCREDIBLY GRAPHIC VIOLENCE CHAPTER, PART 1 (IN FLIP-O-RAMA™)

PILKEY® BRAND O-RAMA

HERE'S HOW IT WORKS!

STEP 1

First, place your *left* hand inside the dotted lines marked "LEFT HAND HERE". Hold the book open *flat*.

STEP 2

Grasp the *right-hand* page with your right thumb and index finger (inside the dotted lines marked "RIGHT THUMB HERE").

STEP 3

Now *quickly* flip the right-hand page back and forth until the picture appears to be *animated*.

(For extra fun, try adding your own sound-effects!)

FLIP-O-RAMA 1

(pages 143 and 145)

Remember, flip *only* page 143.
While you are flipping, be sure you
can see the picture on page 143
and the one on page 145.
If you flip quickly, the two
pictures will start to look like
<u>one</u> *animated* picture.

Don't forget to
add your own sound-effects!

LEFT HAND HERE

THE FIRST TIME
EVER I PUNCHED
YOUR FACE

RIGHT
THUMB
HERE

RIGHT
INDEX
FINGER
HERE

THE FIRST TIME
EVER I PUNCHED
YOUR FACE

FLIP-O-RAMA 2

(pages 147 and 149)

Remember, flip *only* page 147.
While you are flipping, be sure you
can see the picture on page 147
and the one on page 149.
If you flip quickly, the two
pictures will start to look like
<u>one</u> *animated* picture.

Don't forget to
add your own sound-effects!

LEFT HAND HERE

KILLING ME SOFTLY
WITH HIS KONG

147

RIGHT
THUMB
HERE

RIGHT
INDEX
FINGER
HERE

KILLING ME SOFTLY
WITH HIS KONG

CHAPTER 28

DON'T GO BREAKING MY SPINE

With the help of his Stinky-Kong 2000 Mecha-Suit, Mr Meaner was victorious. He picked up Old George and Old Harold in his mighty metallic fist and began to squeeze.

"Hey, don't kill those guys," cried Mr Krupp, as he dried his face on an old red towel with black dots on it. "You'll ruin my lawn!"

"He–he just dried his face!" Old Harold gasped. "Now's our chance!"

Old George and Old Harold reached out
weakly and snapped their fingers.

SNAP! SNAP!

Suddenly, a silly smile spread across Mr
Krupp's freshly dried face.

Quickly, he tore off his clothes and tied his red towel around his neck. The battle of the century was about to begin.

CHAPTER 29

THE INCREDIBLY GRAPHIC VIOLENCE CHAPTER, PART 2 (IN FLIP-O-RAMA™)

FLIP-O-RAMA 3

(pages 155 and 157)

Remember, flip *only* page 155.
While you are flipping, be sure you
can see the picture on page 155
and the one on page 157.
If you flip quickly, the two
pictures will start to look like
<u>one</u> *animated* picture.

Don't forget to
add your own sound-effects!

LEFT HAND HERE

SOMEBODY DONE SOMEBODY'S KONG WRONG

RIGHT
THUMB
HERE

RIGHT
INDEX
FINGER
HERE

SOMEBODY DONE SOMEBODY'S KONG WRONG

FLIP-O-RAMA 4

(pages 159 and 161)

Remember, flip *only* page 159.
While you are flipping, be sure you
can see the picture on page 159
and the one on page 161.
If you flip quickly, the two
pictures will start to look like
<u>one</u> *animated* picture.

Don't forget to
add your own sound-effects!

LEFT HAND HERE

I FIGHT THE KONGS
THAT MAKE THE WHOLE
WORLD STINK

159

RIGHT THUMB HERE

I FIGHT THE KONGS
THAT MAKE THE WHOLE
WORLD STINK

CHAPTER 30
PIQUA PRISON BLUES

The Stinky-Kong 2000 Mecha-Suit was destroyed, and soon Mr Meaner found himself sitting in a cell at Piqua State Penitentiary. Warden Gordon Bordon Schmorden stopped by to have a word with Mr Meaner.

"Well, well, well," said Warden Schmorden smugly. "It looks like your days of giving orders to people are OVER!"

"Go make me an egg-salad sandwich," said Mr Meaner.

"OK," said Warden Schmorden. "Coming right up!"

"And don't forget the dill-pickle relish!" said Mr Meaner.

"I wouldn't dream of forgetting that, sir," said Warden Schmorden.

Five minutes later, Warden Gordon
Bordon Schmorden returned with a lovely
egg-salad sandwich loaded with dill-pickle
relish. Mr Meaner grabbed it and scarfed it
all down.

Suddenly, Mr Meaner's body began to
change. The mayonnaise and the dill-pickle
relish began to combine with the Zygo-
Gogozizzle 24 that had taken over Mr
Meaner's body. First, he began to vibrate and
glow, as tiny sparks of electricity shot out of
his fingers and toes. Then he started growing.

Mr Meaner grew and grew and grew to such a gigantic size, he crashed out of his cell and pushed his way through the side of the jail.

Mr Meaner had transformed into a highly intelligent blob of pure energy.

"I AM SIR STINKS-A-LOT!" he bellowed, as he zapped everything around him with cataclysmic crackles of electricity.

CHAPTER 31
OOZE ON DOWN THE ROAD

Sir Stinks-A-Lot slithered sloppily down the street looking for sweet, sweet revenge.

"Captain Underpants," he called mockingly, "come out and *PLAY-YAY*!"

Suddenly, Captain Underpants swooped in and smashed Sir Stinks-A-Lot right on the noggin with a telephone pole.

The gigantic, evil blob zapped his lightning rays and swung his mighty fists, but Captain Underpants was just too quick.

Old George and Old Harold stood on the sidelines, cheering for the Waistband Warrior.

"Get him, Captain Underpants!" shouted Old George.

"Let's win this thing so we can all go home!" shouted Old Harold.

Sir Stinks-A-Lot was getting very frustrated and annoyed. Then he thought of something really smart.

"Those two guys *seem* to know Captain Underpants pretty well," said Sir Stinks-A-Lot to himself. "I think it's time to find out EXACTLY what they know!"

Sir Stinks-A-Lot raised his terrifying fist above Old George and Old Harold. . .

. . . then clobbered them with a powerful punch.

Quickly, the energy inside Sir Stinks-A-Lot's body began to absorb Old George and Old Harold. The two old friends began to merge with the evil glob of energy, and soon the three had become one.

"HAW! HAW! HAW!" laughed Sir Stinks-A-Lot. "I've absorbed their bodies AND their memories. Soon I'll know everything that THEY know!"

Sir Stinks-A-Lot used his massive, glowing brain to quickly sort through Old George's and Old Harold's memories. He learned how they first met, he learned how they became friends, and he learned how they created Captain Underpants. Unfortunately, Sir Stinks-A-Lot also learned how to *DESTROY* Captain Underpants.

A sinister sneer stretched across the blobby face of the supremely intelligent super-villain. Swiftly, he oozed over to Franz Pond, chuckling maniacally to himself.

"You'd better let those guys go," shouted Captain Underpants, "or I'm gonna—"

"You're not going to do ANYTHING!" screamed Sir Stinks-A-Lot, as he swooshed his mighty hand into the pond and sent a gigantic splash of water flying into the air.

CHAPTER 32

THE NIGHT THE LIGHTS WENT OUT IN PIQUA

The massive spray of water hit Captain Underpants with a powerful *ker-splooosh*. Suddenly, our hero's confidence disappeared, and he fell screaming from the sky.

"AAAAAAAhhh!" he shrieked, as he tumbled to the ground and smashed into the earth with a terrifying sound-effect.

"Hey! I'm OK!" said Mr Krupp, as he sat up and dusted himself off.

"Wait a minute," shouted Sir Stinks-A-Lot. "He's not even *hurt*! How could that be?!!?"

Sir Stinks-A-Lot reached down and touched Mr Krupp with one of his gigantic, glowing fingers. A powerful burst of Zygo-Gogozizzlistic energy zapped forth from his massive fingertip and scanned Mr Krupp's body. Quickly, the villain's bulbous brain analysed each and every strand of DNA in Mr Krupp's body until a foreign substance was detected.

"SO!" shouted Sir Stinks-A-Lot. "You've got alien *Super Power Juice* in your DNA! I guess I'll just have to extract it!"

Sir Stinks-A-Lot's finger grew brighter
and brighter as he performed one of the most
complicated laser surgeries ever: a Super-
Power-Juice-*ectomy*. Carefully, he removed
all of the super-powered elements from Mr
Krupp's DNA and absorbed them all into his
massive, glowing body.

Mr Krupp was unharmed, but he ran
home screaming anyway.

"Now I'VE got super powers!" laughed
Sir Stinks-A-Lot. "And now, I am truly
unstoppable!"

CHAPTER 33

I'M SENDIN' OUT GOOD VIBRATIONS

What Sir Stinks-A-Lot failed to realize, however, was that Old George and Old Harold were still a part of him. Since they had all merged together, the two best friends' brains were now filled with super-powered Zygo-Gogozizzle 24.

It wasn't long before Old George and Old Harold had sorted through every particle of Zygo-Gogozizzle 24 and every glowing joule of energy that made up their hulkingly monstrous body.

Soon they knew everything, from the chemical make-up of their arch-enemy to the events that led to the destruction of Smart Earth. Old George and Old Harold oozed up from the back of Sir Stinks-A-Lot's head and started sending a message.

The two old friends thought as hard as they could, and soon, a telepathic signal radiated from their gooey heads to their old tree house, miles away.

Unfortunately, George and Harold were sound asleep. They didn't pick up the telepathic message at all.

Luckily, someone else did!

Tony, Orlando and Dawn swooshed out of the tree house and headed for a nearby shopping centre. The fate of the entire planet was in their tiny paws.

Sir Stinks-A-Lot had been victorious, and now it was time to gloat. "I've just defeated the world's greatest superhero! And now I'm the most intelligent, most powerful entity the world has ever SEEN!"

He oozed over to his Rid-O-Kid 2000™ factory and kissed it gently on the roof. "Soon, my stinky spray will take over the brains of all the children on Earth," he shouted. "I'll be their leader, and they'll gladly obey my every command!"

Sir Stinks-A-Lot threw back his hideously huge head and laughed and laughed and laughed. "HAW! HAW! HAW! HAW! HAW!"

CHAPTER 35

TO MAKE A LONG STORY SHORT

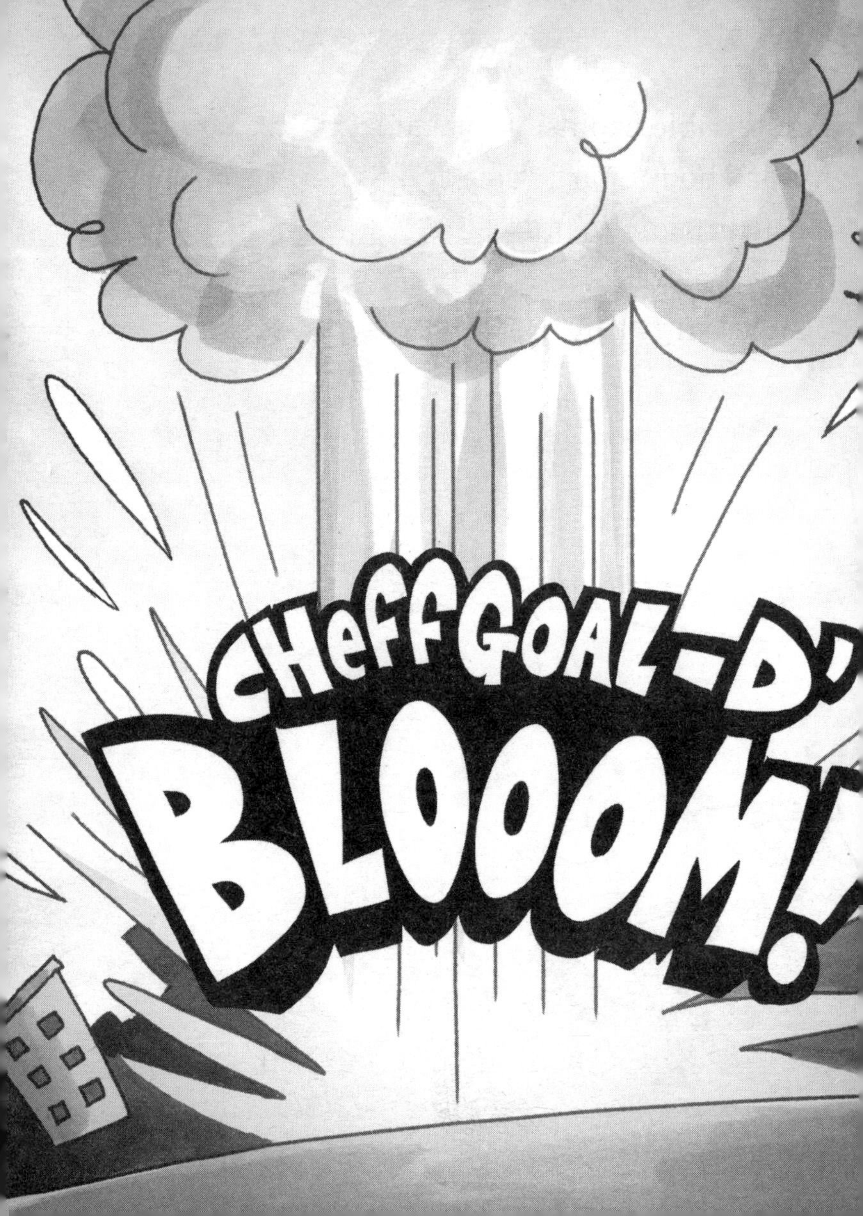

CHAPTER 36

STUCK IN THE PUDDLE WITH YOU

The terrible explosion blasted Sir Stinks-A-Lot's body apart, releasing a powerful electromagnetic pulse and launching the Super Power Juice and the Zygo-Gogozizzle 24 deep into outer space.

The factory was destroyed. The Rid-O-Kid
2000™ had disintegrated, and all that was left
was a big, stinky mess.

A crowd of people gathered around Franz
Pond to view the horrible glob of devastation.

Suddenly, the glob began to bubble and move. Then, Old George and Old Harold climbed out of its gooey centre. They were completely unharmed.

"Hooray!" shouted the crowd of people.

The glob began to bubble and move again. All at once, Tony, Orlando and Dawn popped out. They were fine, also.

"Yippee!" cheered the crowd of people.

Finally, the glob bubbled and moved one last time, and Mr Meaner popped his head out. He was back to his old self, too.

"Awwww, MAAAN!" moaned the crowd of people.

CHAPTER 37
BACK TO NORMAL

George and Harold woke up to the rising sun and looked out their tree house window.

"The whole city looks like it's back to normal," said George.

"Even the stinky brown clouds have disappeared!" said Harold.

It was a good thing, too, because George's and Harold's colds had finally gone away.

The two friends climbed down from their tree house and looked in Harold's bedroom window. Yesterday Harold was still sound asleep. Soon, the Rid-O-Kid 2000™ would wear off, and Yesterday George and Yesterday Harold would be back to normal.

George and Harold walked out to the front garden, where they saw some familiar faces.

"What happened?" cried Harold. "Is everything OK?"

"Of course it is," said Old George.

"Yeah," said Old Harold. "Adults can be heroes, too, you know!"

Old George and Old Harold told their younger selves all about their great adventure while they walked towards Echo Hills together.

On the way, they passed Mr Krupp. He was outside in his garden raking the grass as a jogger ran by snapping her fingers.

SNAP! SNAP! SNAP! SNAP! SNAP! SNAP!

"You stay away from my garden!" Mr Krupp shouted.

"What's going on?" cried Harold. "Mr Krupp just heard somebody snap their fingers, and he DIDN'T turn into you-know-who!"

"I have no idea how that happened," said Old George.

Perhaps it was the electromagnetic pulse that erased the hypnotic spell from Mr Krupp's brain. Or maybe it happened during the Super-Power-Juice-*ectomy*. Nobody knew for sure, but for some strange reason, Mr Krupp was now back to normal, too.

Soon our heroes arrived at Echo Hills and prepared to return to the future.

"Thanks for all of your help last night," said George.

"Yeah," said Harold. "You guys did a pretty good job – for old people."

"PRETTY GOOD?!!?" cried Old Harold.

"OLD PEOPLE?!!?" cried Old George.

CHAPTER 38

HOME AGAIN, NATURALLY

Suddenly, there was a blinding flash of light. Twenty years flashed forward in an instant, and the empty hilltop was now filled with homes and trees. Old George's and Old Harold's families were all there, too, anxiously waiting for their return.

It was a joyful reunion.

"Well," said Harold, "I think we'd better go back home."

"You know," said George, "we don't actually *have* to go home."

"What do you mean?" asked Harold.

"We've got our own time machine," said George. "We could go anywhere we want! We can explore time together. We can go on awesome new adventures!"

"Wow!" said Harold. "That sounds like fun!"

"What should we do first?" asked Harold.

"Let's go rescue Crackers and Sulu,"
said George. The three baby hamsterdactyls
flapped their wings with excitement.

"How in the world are we ever going to do
that?" asked Harold.

"We'll figure something out," said George,
as he set the controllers. "We always do!"

George and Harold and their happy pets
waved goodbye to their future families, and
together they all disappeared into a ball of
brilliant light.

CHAPTER 39

MEANWHILE,
BACK IN THE PRESENT. . .

A few hours had passed, and the Rid-O-Kid 2000™ had finally worn off.

Yesterday George and Yesterday Harold were back to their old selves again, but nothing around them seemed normal at all.

"I wonder where George and Harold went," said Yesterday George.

"I have no idea," said Yesterday Harold.

"And where did Tony, Orlando and Dawn go?" asked Yesterday George.

"Beats me," said Yesterday Harold. "It seems like they just disappeared."

Yesterday George and Yesterday Harold didn't know what had happened, or why everything had turned out OK. But it seemed like things were going to be just fine from now on, and they were very grateful.

"Well, what should we do now?" asked Harold.

"Let's make a new comic book," said George.

"About Captain Underpants?" asked Harold.

"Nah," said George. "Let's do something different. How about a Dog Man comic?"

"OK," said Harold happily.

And together, the two friends
wrote and drew and laughed
all afternoon.

HAVE YOU READ
YOUR UNDERPANTS TODAY

CHECK OUT THE APP!

Available on the **App Store**

COMING NEXT
From George and Harold

The Graphic Novel That Started it all!

THE ADVENTURES OF
DOG MAN
The World's Greatest cop

Tree House Comix

ACTION 'N' LAFFS!

IN FULL COLOR!

FLIP-O-RAMA in every chapter!

THE FOURTH EPIC NOVEL BY GEORGE BEARD AND HAROLD HUTCHINS

when we were in kindergarten, we made up our First Hero Ever: Dog Man!

me too!

Next year, Dog Man will star in his first Full-Length Graphic Novel!!!

Laugh Your tails off!!!

DOG MAN

Read it to your dog!!!

and then...

DOG MAN

Fetch your copy soon!!!

mBLFF!

DOG MAN

2016 is the YEAR of the DOG, MAN!

ABOUT THE AUTHOR

When Dav Pilkey was a kid, he suffered from ADHD, dyslexia and behavioural problems. Dav was so disruptive in class that his teachers made him sit out in the hall every day. Fortunately, Dav loved to draw and make up stories. He spent his time in the hallway creating his own original comic books.

In the second grade, Dav Pilkey created a comic book about a superhero named Captain Underpants. His teacher ripped it up and told him he couldn't spend the rest of his life making silly books.

Fortunately, Dav was not a very good listener.